Everything is Magic

By

Gary Lee Parsley II

Table of Contents

Battle for a Dying World!

Battle For a Dying World

1.

There is a reason why a polar shift has never been documented. as it would likely destroy most life on the planet, and certainly civilization as we know it. The magnetic forces involved would produce an effect so cataclysmic as to reduce humanity to living in caves. But this story isn't about all of that. It's just another day of school in a small European village. All the kids are werewolves, but they still go to school because it's safe because it's daytime. But then boom, polar shift. There's the moon. Half the little brats grow teeth and fur and then just start eating everybody. The teacher is trying to fight them away with a ruler, until his hand gets chomped off and then his face.

"Oh, why couldn't it have happened during naptime?"

2.

The tiny werewolves won the day. The entire village was a bloody slaughter. Meanwhile deep beneath the earth in a secret laboratory. The evil wizard continued to harness the power of collapsing super clusters. His ingenious plan to rule the world with dark matter was nearly complete. Little did he know however that his plans would be spoiled when mutant spiders slithered in through cracks in the wall and ate his brains. Then his mad assistant gathered up the important things and stole away into the night. He went to his friend's house. She was sitting on the porch eating food and skinning a possum.

"Get in," he said, "It's urgent, and scientific." Not wanting to be a wet blanket she agreed and climbed aboard.

Off they sped by moonlight. on and on until dawn they fled. He didn't dare stop to rest. He knew they would be looking for him.

3.

They entered a small diner. The waitress was grouchy, but they ordered things to eat and began to discuss their plans. They did not notice the fellow with the dark hat and sunglasses who was reading a newspaper across the way. Not until he stood up and opened fire with machine guns. Many brains were splattered and a few fingers were blown off. The man in the hat screamed, then grabbed the case, leapt over a table and exited, but not before tossing a couple of grenades over his shoulder. Outside he slid behind the wheel of a black sports car. As the diner burst into flames the car burned rubber and fishtailed out onto the roadway. The man then dialled his phone and waited. After a moment it was answered. He reported that the targets were down and the package was secure. Then he lit a cigarette and turned on the radio. Nothing but news of the polar shift on every station. He clicked off the radio and began to hum.

4.

Outside the diner the time traveler watched as the car drove away. Carefully he crept through the wreckage finding the assistant barely conscious and clinging to life.

"Sorry about your friend," he said.

The mad assistant cackled through the blood.

"Perhaps," he said, "But it's the device you've come for."

The traveller did not reply he held out his hand the assistant reached beneath his coat and produced an object no bigger than a cigarette pack.

"I take it you know what to do with this," he said.

"I don't," replied the traveller. "But I know someone who will."

One last pained chuckle escaped before the mad assistant released his hold on the mysterious device. Then he died, the traveller placed it in his own pocket, tapped a button on a keypad on his wrist, and then vanished.

5.

High above the earth aboard his private space station, the mastermind observed all the events he had set in motion comfortably behind a bank of screens and monitors. Things were running smoothly. The repeated interferences of the time traveller were disturbing, but should not affect the overall outcome of his grand plans or so he was thinking as he reached for his drink. Not paying attention he blundered, spilling the contents across the expensive and delicate hardware. Sparks erupted and a fire broke out. He shouted for assistance as he beat at the flames with the sleeves of his jacket. Inadvertantly he hit the button for the airlock. His last thoughts as he and his crew were jettisoned out into the vacuum of space were of what a foolish place that was for that button.

6.

The polar shift had done a lot more than disrupt the schooling of a town full of werewolves. The destruction and havoc were worldwide. Oceans had escaped their boundaries, flooding entire regions. Monstrous mountains of water invading coastlines and continuing in across hundreds of miles of unsuspecting landscape. Power grids were down, and communications shut off. The air currents seemed to have gone insane as well. The entire skin of the world was attempting to restabalize after the violent twist of the underlying core. People were not happy. Climates were altered, buildings & planes were down everywhere. Earthquakes and fires raging out of control, no one was unaffected. Save for some soldiers in an underground base, and their superiors orbiting high above on the space station. There were survivors, however. Huddled together here and there, with no power and little food. Many of them thought this might be the end for the human race. Something else was different too. It had started as a feeling many of them dismissed as shock. After a while though it became undeniable. Something had awakened in their minds. Something very old, and very intriguing.

7.

His joints were stiff and his back ached, how long had he been shut up in this cupboard? Was there any chance the sun had returned and the monsters were gone? It seemed quieter. Ever so cautiously he eased open the door. Indeed, the sun was shining, but upon such horrors as he had never witnessed in his long life. The cafeteria was strewn end to end with gore, the devils had danced the unnatural night away. Pieces of children and adults alike lay everywhere. The walls were decorated with the last efforts of their struggles.

"Hello," he shouted. "Is anyone there?" no answer.

Nervously he crept from room to room, down the hall and to the front door. Cold, why was it so damned cold. The door seemed stuck, he pushed harder and as it gave way he was greeted with a blast of even colder air. To his further astonishment, the ground outside was covered with snow.

"Snow by god, in July. The world had gone mad."

Running to the lot for his car he began to be aware of strange voices in his head. Sounds as well as images. He started the car and tried to clear his mind. The radio was telling the most unbelievable story of a worldwide cataclysm. It couldn't be true. But as he looked around and recalled the events of the night before, he knew that it must be.

8.

While a great many of the earth's inhabitants were pulling their hair out, wailing, sobbing, and questioning their plight, not everyone had succumbed to the certainty of doom. They gathered together, around generators, and weapons. Pooled food and other resources. In general, they tried to make sense of what had happened, and of what was to become of them. One of the oddest things was the visions. Like a song in one's head. More pronounced in some not so much in others. Some went mad from it, while to some it was like an awakening of sorts. No one thought much of it until one night at a regular gathering when a girl stepped forward and announced that the energy had communicated to her a way to move objects with her mind. Strangely, no one laughed. Apparently, she wasn't the only one with whom the energy had been communicating. Most could read minds to some extent. Some could move things, and a few could start fires.

"It's witchcraft!" exclaimed some. "A gift from god," claimed others. Whatever the case, a new age of sorcery had begun.

9.

A few aeons ago, there once existed a world much like our own. Sentient beings attempted time and again to create and sustain a civilization. After a few botched attempts they eventually cobbled together something that seemed to work for everyone and for about 20,000 years they flourished. In that time, they discovered many wonderful and useful ways to amuse themselves. One of these was exploring and colonizing nearby planets. This was a most fortunate endeavour. For one day, seemingly normal as any other, their planet began to tremble. As witnessed from a nearby space station, the planet burst open and from it, bathed in the flames of their wasted home, was a creature. So wretched, so horrifying it was that the mere sight of it caused many to immediately lose their minds. As the creature vanished into the depths of space, the survivors aboard the space station noticed an odd thing. They could no longer read each other's thoughts.

10.

The general sat at his desk deep inside the bunker and wondered what else could go wrong. That idiot scientist had jumped the gun, the event had occurred ahead of schedule. His assistant had escaped with the device and the man he had sent to retrieve it had been duped at least he was safe down here, surrounded by 10 thousand men and 2 miles of earth. For some reason, he was unable to make contact with his superiors up on the space station. Probably some sort of interference due to the effects of the event. He would hear from them soon enough. For now, he had plenty to deal with. Some of the men had been developing strange symptoms, hearing voices, and hallucinating. All cards on the table, he had to admit to experiencing a bit of odd phenomena himself.

11.

He stood by the tall window, back straight, hands clasped behind his back. He squinted his eyes as the bursts from the retro rockets lit up the base, and slowed the descent of the great approaching ship. This was to be the first of many. The host had been disturbed and the early stages of evacuations had begun. If something was not done soon this base would become the temporary home for the refugees of the planet recently known as Earth.

"True, this was a worst-case scenario."

The cities on Mars Venus and Titan could sustain survivors for a time but without supply runs to Earth, it was doubtful they would survive the 82 years until the next expected contact from the fleet. As he walked toward the gate to meet with the ship's captain, he wondered just how close they had come. The creature had stirred once before 50 years ago under the rain of nukes being tested. How it had slept through the polar shift; he could not imagine. Any further disturbance, well he had seen the results of that firsthand.

12.

She awoke slowly. A strange taste in her mouth. It had to be a dream, right? Just another day at school and then that strange earthquake. Suddenly it had gotten dark. The moon was out. It was one thing for the change to happen at home, where it was safe. Out on the fields where the goats roamed, but people knew better. Of course, she knew better, than to ever be near to town when the cycle was coming, but it had happened so fast and she wasn't the only one. There were half a dozen in her class alone not to mention a few of the teachers.

"Where was she now?" she looked around trying to get her bearings. Her clothes were in rags and smeared with blood, she was cold.

"How could it possibly be snowing?" something had happened. She had to get home. She wrapped what was left of her garments around her as tightly as she could and began to walk toward what, she did not know.

13.

Being for the most part not terribly honest creatures, the introduction of true telepathy can be at first quite unnerving to most. Being unable to mask their inner hearts people began to become nervous around one another. Many sought solitude. Even close friends and family upon discovering each other's baser natures, found it difficult to associate with or even communicate. The initial shock of it did die down eventually. They had after all survived something horrific together. They would need to remain united if they were to survive. Groups began to form around the movers and the fire starters, and sects arose of people who tried to renounce the new gifts. It seemed there would be no end to the conflict. Fortunately, with most of the population destroyed, there was abundant space and resources for the groups to spread out and adjust to these changes in their own ways. As to why these new abilities had developed it seemed no one knew. Certainly, it was related to the event, but how?

14.

After having their home world destroyed, and surviving for many centuries aboard star ships, moon bases, and a few worlds they had managed to terraform and colonize. They began to search for a new world more like their original planet. Stories of how the world was destroyed were distorted over time until few believed there ever had been a creature. As the race spread itself across galaxy after galaxy, the tale became more myth than truth. Until they discovered another planet suffering a similar if not the same infestation. Not long after settling in this place, the ages-lost abilities began to return. Carefully they began to probe into the planet trying to discern if it could in fact be infected by yet another such abominable creature. In their efforts the beast was unintentionally disturbed and fled, destroying yet another perfectly inhabitable world. They tracked the beast from a distance as it searched for a new place to rest. Tirelessly it moved from system to system until at last, finding a suitable nest it burrowed in and began its slumber. Patiently they watched and waited until the planet had become stable. Returning once every hundred or so years to check the progress. If they could find a way to live here without disturbing the creature, they could finally have the home they had been searching for.

15.

This was even better than he could have hoped for. The plan had been to hold the world hostage under the threat of the polar shit. For whatever reason, the damn fool had just gone ahead and pulled the trigger. He had hoped to rule over nations, now the world was his for the taking. The general looked out over his troops, now assembled on the training grounds. The telepathy which had been a problem, had become an asset. Communication was instant, each knew the other's thoughts. No unit had ever functioned so smoothly in the history of combat. And now, while the world was still reeling, still trying to put itself back together after the worst disaster in the history of mankind. Now, he would take control of what was left. Who could challenge him, who could possibly deny him, he had had no contact from the space station, something had happened. Nothing they could do from up there anyway. This was his show now. As the first of the units began to roll out, he thought to himself,

"It's just the way it should be."

16.

While the food was not all that scarce, problems such as locating it, storing it and distributing it did arise. It was difficult to keep people in charge of these things. Leadership is hard enough without people knowing your every guarded thought while you may be trying to help, your own selfish motives are right out in the open for all to see, it just gets tiresome. Groups disbanded, and more people broke away and decided to have a go at making it on their own. The groups that did stay together were often like-minded criminals. When selfish motives are the norm, it just becomes a power struggle and powerful people it seemed were springing up everywhere. As bad as it seemed, there were more than a few groups who managed to stay banded together despite or perhaps because of the telepathy. Through them, the spark of civilization would live on. Rumors however had begun to spread, of a powerful group, of armed soldiers with tanks, taking over smaller groups wherever they went, any who tried to resist did not resist for long.

17.

Of course, the tribes had tried to make war with the visitors. Some adored them while others feared them, but no one understood who they were, where they had come from, or what they wanted. They weren't all good or bad, but over the centuries they had revealed their humanity in just about every way imaginable. Slaves to some, pets to others a few who believed we might one day be equals. As human society developed, the ancients gradually faded into obscurity while still controlling and maintaining a certain status quo, they found it was just easier to, for the most part, keep their existence a closely guarded secret. Mostly they let the Earth people continue on as they normally would, the planet was large enough after all. The one thing they could not abide by was anything that might disturb the slumber of the creature. If disturbed, it would flee destroying the world it left behind and everything on it. Now the unthinkable had happened in their quest for power, they had caused a cataclysm so immense, that it was a wonder that the beast slept on. They had given the humans too much freedom, a mistake they did not plan to repeat.

18.

It had started with a hum. Faint at first, then growing, as it grew the ground began to shake, violently at first, growing even more so. Then the slip, a crack like a shot as the ground itself broke the speed of sound. That anyone survived at all is a testament to the luck if not resiliency of the human race then the settling. The plates and then the seas, smoke and ash from giant volcanoes blanketed entire regions. The atmosphere was disturbed as it was churned up and dropped here and there. Massive storms were formed by the rapid heating and cooling of air that was whipping around uncontrollably. Planes crashing, ships sinking, cities being toppled and even swallowed up by the convulsing earth. No one was prepared for the full devastation that was wrought. Even the wizard began to second-guess his chances at survival. As the dust settled and the fortunate began to peek out from the debris, the monster stirred momentarily. It occurred to him he should probably move but he was old and so tired. Soon he thought, but slumbered on.

19.

With the majority of their population relocated to off-world outposts, they could now turn their attention to the matter at hand. The humans. First things first they would track down the technology which had caused this near catastrophe, second, the remaining humans would be rounded up and organized. Not only were they unwilling to share the planet, but they had seemed determined to destroy it for some time and they had nearly succeeded. A significant force would be deployed on each continent. Being more familiar with the abilities derived from proximity to the beast gave them an advantage. Not that it would be needed they possessed all the technology a 50000-year-old civilization might be expected to have. The idea was to quickly overwhelm and subdue the native race forcing them to submit. Some resistance was to be expected. However, as with most well-thought-out plans, there were things they did not think of.

20.

And so they battled on, for decades the two races struggled for domination of the planet. Factions arose and fell. At times the two races would unite, in order to take down a more sinister entity. Temporary peace was achieved time and again, only to be broken when one side could not be constrained to the accord of the other. Occasionally, the beast would revel in the dreams of men. These dreams he did not quite understand for he dreamed only of warmth and of peace and uninterrupted slumber. Indeed, it was only a matter of time before the torrents that raged on the surface of his happy cocoon caused him to sense the danger. Like so many times before he decided he would need to move on to find a quieter place.

At the end of the hundred-year cycle. The travellers returned to find what they had hoped to be their new home, a smouldering field of burned-out space dust. They gathered up the surviving refugees on the surrounding worlds which surprisingly enough consisted of a few native earth people. They carefully tracked the trajectory in which the beast had headed and set off to find their next hope of finding a new world to call home.

Marvel And Terror

1.

He used to be somebody, some big shot, up on the surface. Back in the old world.

She'd never wanted servants and had much enjoyed the solitude offered here. It was terribly expensive and for a while had hardly seemed worth it to most. So deserted for such a time that it had nearly, haha, gone under.

Then the bugs had come. Whether it was a natural cycle, or caused by global warming no one knew. Either way, the surface of the world had changed in a matter of days to a place unrecognizable and nearly uninhabitable.

Of course, as massive as it was, and even with the massive new editions, there wasn't room for everyone. Meant to comfortably sustain around 50,000, the population of Ocean City was now over 100,000 and growing by the day. And so, Hank and his small family had become her charges.

There was plenty for them to do, and she did not mind the help, but she did enjoy her solitude, which had become practically nonexistent. She couldn't complain too much, she had seen a video of what had become of the surface world, and she did feel some pity for the refugees.

At least down here she was somebody. She was a tenant and not just any tenant. She'd been one of the original tenants, and also an investor. One could say she owned a part of Ocean City, and by extension, a great majority of the now inhabitable world.

2.

How they had laughed at the idea of an underwater city. Accused him of wasting billions on something so trivial. Nothing more than a novelty they had said. Ashamed to admit it but at first, he had been delighted to see them come banging at the door. Until the harsh reality of the horrors of the surface world had sunk in.

Then of course he had no choice but to do his best to save as many as he could. But at what cost? The storerooms were plentiful, but not endless. The air filtration systems were working over to accommodate this many. Teams were working to expand, but things took time. Every day more arrived pleading to be granted sanctuary.

How it pained him to watch them burn alive just beyond the gates. but what could he do? They were jammed in like sardines as it was. Many had been integrated into the existing population, but more were left to camp out in the commons and roam the many tunnels.

Ships came sometimes, but many did not want to risk even that. Nowhere above ground was completely safe. He had to wonder, would it ever stabilise? Would this be the end of humanity?

3.

Considering that the life span of a fly is about one day, while a human who lives to be 100 will have lived well over 30,000 days, it is not inconceivable that there could be creatures on this earth who maybe took a nap and awoke to find the place overrun with humans. This is an estimation of what happened with the creatures who became known mainly as, the bugs.

Resembling wasps and other winged insects, ranging in size from 6 inches to a few species more than 100 ft long. They lay

16

dormant, hibernating, under the crust of the earth for thousands of years. Not only surviving the immense temperatures and pressure but seeming to desire it.

As hives of these creatures began to erupt all around the globe at approximately the same time. Scientists could only speculate as to the cause. No one got to ponder the question for very long, as the atmosphere was soon filled with them.

Each one was hot enough to burn for hours before returning to the magma from which they had sprung. Everything they touched was set ablaze, which only attracted more of them.

Cities burned in hours. Crops were destroyed, and forests were decimated. They used so much oxygen that it became difficult to breathe around them.

To astronauts watching from space it seemed the entire earth had been set ablaze. Eventually, the smoke and ash muddied the atmosphere and the once beautiful blue and green marble became mostly grey with patches of fiery orange and red.

4.

They had huddled here and there in holes in the ground. In basements and tunnels and caves, anywhere it seemed the bugs might not find them. They tried to make plans and provisions, yet over them, all hung a blanket of despair and uncertainty. Whatever safety they had found could only be temporary.

They seemed to be more active during the day, which inspired some of the braver souls to attempt scavenger missions after sundown. Sometimes they would succeed in finding food, water, and other essentials. Other times they would not. Communication was limited, but word had spread of safe zones. Ocean City had already taken on more refugees than they could sustain, but the word of a military base deep under the mountains had become a thing for the hopeful to latch onto.

The bugs were not indestructible. In fact, once you got past the immense heat, they were actually no more durable than most insectoids.

People found shovels and aluminium bats to be quite effective. The guns worked fine, but the sound drew more. One or two could cause a good bit of damage, but the real danger was in being swarmed. Patiently they waited out the sweltering stretch of the day, and when night fell, they set out for the mountain.

5.

Not all of Ocean City was underwater. First, there was the surrounding suburban area, mostly populated by workers who commuted to their various jobs via the train system. The expansive greeting and observation centre served as the main entrance as well as being a tourist attraction which celebrated a tremendous view of the city both above and below the waves.

Then a system of tunnels and elevators led down to the city itself, which was comprised of 37 underwater structures. Some are spread out over acres and acres, while others resemble typical buildings. A few of them even break the surface and rise high above the water. All are interconnected by tunnels for walking, some vehicles, and of course the train system.

Most buildings feature moon pools where submersible vehicles are kept and launched. Seafloor roadways are marked by a series of lights leading to such sights as the coral reef, a sunken ship, and the edge of the shelf on which the city rests.

Most of the domestic areas are quite luxuriant, due to the fact that they were designed to cater to mostly high-end clientele. Even most of the lower suites boast state-of-the-art A.I. systems to monitor temperature, air quality, and pressure.

The city took six years to build, and billions of dollars. Many found the idea fascinating but not terribly important. How wrong they all were?

6.

The coast had been clear when we had entered the building. We moved swiftly and quietly, but somehow the wretched things had been alerted to our presence. Jack had made a run for it. He was pretty good at fighting them off, but after bashing a few of them with the pipe he carried they had swarmed him.

He pulled out the sawed-off and took out a few more, but by that time they were all over him. The sound of his screams as they sunk into their giant radioactive stingers was hardly bearable. He went down in a ball of flames still trying to slash at them with his knife.

We didn't hesitate to use the distraction to our advantage. We'd all liked Jack, but there was nothing we could do for him now.

There were six of us then. We moved as quietly as we could toward an abandoned house. It wouldn't be any better than the store if we were seen. The bastards incinerated anything they touched. It was a miracle there were any standing structures at all.

We'd almost reached the house when Louis tripped over something and went headlong across the pavement. He immediately knew he was a goner and did the right thing by drawing their attention away from us.

"Poor Louis, He was a good dude," and he went out guns blazing.

It's hard to watch anyone go down like that, to be completely helpless to do anything for them. We made the house and waited it out until the swarm moved on.

We made it back to the camp just before dawn. We had a pretty good haul, but it was hard to feel good about. Seemed every time we went out, we lost someone. How long till there was no one left to go?

7.

At first, they never ventured out over the water. You could stand by the windows of the tower and watch helplessly as the world burned. More and more though they were making the journey. Apparently curious about the shiny thing out on the water.

We had killed all the lights so as to not draw their attention. Yet somehow, by smell or perhaps heat, they had become more and more aware of our presence.

Small ones at first. The building was steel and glass, engineered to withstand hurricane-force wind and waves. There seemed little chance of them breaking through. Still, it was horrifying to watch them scuttle across the glass. Leaving burnt smudges as they did so.

Then the larger ones had begun to arrive. Some the size of dogs, or small deer. This caused quite a panic. No one knew how big they actually got. Sometimes the glass would actually shudder under their weight.

A watch was posted just in case one should break through. Then that floor would have to be evacuated and locked down. The breach would have to be defended until the people could be moved somewhere safe.

The first time it did happen was a disaster. Despite all the planning, it had been chaos. Some ran to escape and others to fight. Several people had been trampled. Dozens were badly burned and several were killed.

There were fewer people in the tower after that. Less apt to be watching out the windows. Not that anything could have been done to stop it, even had we known. The whole building had shaken violently. Most thought it was an earthquake, but no It was the biggest bug any of us had ever seen.

8.

The building shook horribly. The sounds of rending steel and shattering glass paralyzed the hearts of everyone. The beast had to be over fifty feet long. Its gargantuan insectoid feet pierced the sides of the building in several places as it scrabbled for purchase, setting fires and wreaking havoc with casual disdain.

Several of the sentries opened fire on it with automatic weapons. This only made it move around, further weakening the integrity of the structure. Several gazed in disbelief at its enormous curious face as it peered inside looking for food or god knows what.

Even those below could hear and feel the effects of the catastrophe happening above. Leaks began to spring. Cries of the trapped, for the dead and the dying echoed throughout the halls and the tunnels.

It was pandemonium as frightened inhabitants searched furiously for any place that might provide refuge from the impending threats of death and dismemberment rising up on all sides.

Apparently smelling or sensing something desirable, the creature had begun to gnaw at the building with its huge mandibles.

A few remained to make a last stand in defence of the tower. Emptying clip after clip into the creature until eventually it had had enough and moved on in search of less tedious prey.

There was a short-lived moment of triumph. Until the extent of the damage became obvious. The crippled blazing and flooded tower began to crumble. And then fell over into the ocean with a tremendous splash.

The rubble rained down onto the other parts of the city, breaking domes, severing tunnels, and generally making a mess of everything. When the last breached corridor had been sealed off and everyone was as safe as they could hope to be, over 5000 were considered lost and ocean tower was a pile of debris on the ocean floor.

9.

He used to be a nobody. Back before the rest of the world had gone to hell. Before the bugs had awoken from their nap and declared the earth for themselves. Just another cog in a wheel, but that wheel had been Ocean City. And now it seemed it was the only wheel in town.

Just a custodian. No matter how nice a place was it seemed there would still be someone to clean the toilets and shine the floors. But fortune it seemed had smiled on him, for on the day of the awakening he had been nestled safely away. While billionaires burned with their houses, and politicians were devoured along with their armies, he had been deep in the bowels of Ocean City. Changing light bulbs.

How instrumental he had been in those first few days. He knew all the routines and where everything was. Had helped with situating the refugees, and adapting areas for shelters and medical. Giving direction and helping out as needed. How they had looked on him with such gratitude. It was a nice change.

But as days turned into months, the novelty began to wear off. The reality had set in that he may never leave this place. Never walk in the sun or breathe fresh air. His sanctuary would inevitably become his tomb. And so, like most of them, he began to lose hope.

People had been on edge, but since the collapse of the tower, it had become worse. Fights and riots broke out, a rash of suicides, and a few attempts at sabotage. Something good needed to happen, otherwise the inhabitants might begin to tear themselves apart.

But what could he do? Just a lowly custodian. Eager to lend a hand or a smile. But this was a problem that required so much more. Then it came to him.

10.

They had crossed over a hundred miles of charred and barren wasteland. During the course of this, their numbers had progressively dwindled from a few hundred down to around eighty.

It was slow going as they could not move in a large group. Small bands would go out on scavenging and reconnaissance missions and only at night. When they found a suitable place to move to, they would bring them on buses. Specially outfitted with metal screens.

At last, the scouts had reached the gates of the mountain base, they approached with caution, not knowing what to expect. From a distance, they observed a group of soldiers patrolling the perimeter in a tank. Unsure of how to proceed, they bickered amongst themselves.

Eventually, they decided to just be direct and sent out three men to greet them. The soldiers were wary, but not hostile. This was not the first group of survivors to seek refuge in the base. One of them radioed the base and another vehicle came out to receive them.

They were given food and a place to sleep, when they woke, they were met by an officer of some rank, who informed them of the situation of the base. It was already overcrowded. Low on supplies and unsure of how much longer if ever, it might be until more could be attained.

It was after some discussion, agreed that they could bring in the sick the wounded, the very old and young. They were given rations, ammo, and weapons, and sent back to their camp to deliver the news. The base would do what they could but for the most part. They were on their own.

11.

There were more than a few perks to working in Ocean City, one of which was free access to the trams and the tours. He had often enjoyed riding out to the reef aboard the sub with the big glass window in the side.

Since the disaster, the tours have stopped. Everyone had more important things to do. Recently however it was more of a case of no one feeling like doing anything. The feelings of hopelessness and lostness had settled over everyone like a shroud.

Sure, this wouldn't solve all the problems they faced, but it was at least something. The substation was far from being deserted, as with every square inch of Ocean City, it had been renovated to accommodate the refugees. When he announced his intentions to travel out to the reef, he was at first met with jeers and general apathy. He was however determined that this was the thing to do, so he carried on.

He hadn't the first idea about how to pilot a sub and began to feel slightly overwhelmed by all the buttons and levers. A few had gathered out of curiosity, perhaps awaiting further disaster.

Still determined not to be deterred, he began hitting switches at random, until the wonder of all wonders the thing came to life.

Then something happened, people began to board, and soon the craft was filled.

If we're lucky he'll kill us all, said one man. Not as if we've anything better to do said another. And so began the first post-apocalyptic tour of the reef captained by a one-time cleaner of toilets and changer of bulbs.

12.

Ocean City had been many things to many people. It was a vast series of underwater complexes. Boasting posh domiciles and extraordinary office spaces. It had a thriving business in tourism, but it was also the home of a high-tech deep-sea research facility. Its investors were deep-pocketed and possessed of a variety of special interests.

Deep in the lowest sub-levels of the facility scientists were busy, conducting experiments and doing research on a number of special projects which might have met with a bit more skepticism in the world above.

From propulsion systems for submarines and advanced dive equipment to nanotechnology and genetic enhancements for improved free diving. Ocean City had been in the business of living in the ocean since before its foundations had been laid.

Why this obsession with the deep you ask? Aside from the fascination with the natural wonders of our vast seas. It could be that something had been discovered down there. Something which begged further study.

Two-thirds of our world had been essentially off-limits to us for as long as we were consciously aware. What resources might lay just beyond this seemingly impenetrable barrier? And was there a reason for it?

A team of specialists gathered their gear boarded a submarine and set off for a site not listed on any of the tours. They went out to the edge of the shelf and then began the descent toward the giant stone doorway which had been discovered decades before, but was still a well-kept secret from the rest of the world.

What lay behind that door the world might not be ready for, but at this point ready or not, it was time to go through.

13.

Ground penetrating radar had revealed massive empty spaces beyond the great door. It was not known whether or not the compartments were flooded and in case they were not, great pains had been taken to ensure they remained that way. To preserve whatever was inside, or just to make exploration that much easier.

A structure had been built over the exterior of the great door in a place where the wall was revealed to be much thinner. The water had been pumped out and large drilling machines had been brought down and begun the process of making a small human-sized opening. It had been slow going, but finally, they had broken through.

The air inside was breathable and the pressure was tolerable. Miraculously, nearly a mile deep they stepped through the portal onto a dry floor and breathed oxygen.

Quickly they went to work setting up lights and generators. Carefully documenting each step as they went. The interior of the cavern was clearly man-made, or rather, made by something. It certainly wasn't natural. There was little to observe in the first chamber, so they set up a base of operations and readied themselves to push further in.

The deeper they went the more amazed they became. The walls and floors became increasingly more decorated with patterns and designs of great sophistication. Whatever had built these passages had been not only intelligent but also quite creative.

At last, they reached what at first appeared to be a dead end, but no at the end of the chamber stood yet another door. This one was not made of stone. It was metal, and it was covered in a writing that no one alive had ever seen.

14.

He knew it was possible that more than a few of them hoped he might kill them all. That relieved some of the pressure. He'd been on the tour a few times so he was fairly certain he knew the way. However, getting lost was still a strong possibility.

Piloting the craft, however, was unlike anything he had ever attempted. It was quite large for one thing, and would hardly stop on a dime. After a while though he began to get the hang of it and before long, they were headed out toward the reef.

Once they were moving steadily out along the lighted path, the passengers became more relaxed. A few of them even stood gazing out at the ocean floor, perhaps admiring how the sea life just carried on oblivious to the state of the world above. For them, nothing had changed. It was just another day of swimming looking for food and avoiding predators.

"What are we looking at tour guide?" jeered one man.

He then became aware of the microphone which was used by the captain to draw attention to various sights and provide insight into Ocean City for the tourists. Nervously he picked it up and began to speak.

Not a speaker by any means, he expected to be heckled or ridiculed at any moment, but it seemed they weren't paying much attention. Most wrapped deeply in their own thoughts and observations

After they had toured the reef for an hour or so he began to head back.

"I want to see the edge," someone said.

It wasn't like they had to be anywhere so he figured, "Why not." And so off they headed, toward the edge.

As they drew near, he wasn't alone in observing something fairly curious. Another craft, much larger, also headed out toward the edge. Then, to the astonishment of everyone, it continued out over the abyss and began to dive.

15.

Hundreds of thousands of years ago, life on earth had evolved to a degree that would make what we consider sophisticated to appear infantile by comparison. Medicine, government, transportation energy and food problems had all been solved and were taught even to children in grade school. Robotics and electronics had removed the need for physical labour. Money was a thing of the past, if something was done the only incentive was in the doing of it.

Life had flourished in this fashion for thousands of years. They even had ways of defending against asteroids and solar flares. What they weren't prepared for, were the bugs.

Much like us, they had been caught completely unaware. Their civilization had been pushed back into caves and into the deep.

After a few thousand years the ash in the atmosphere had made the surface too cold, and so the bugs had returned to their nest deep in the molten bowels of the earth. The surface however remained uninhabitable for many thousands of years.

The people had become accustomed to living underground. They had hewn great cities from the rock. They had mastered travelling beneath the waves, and through vibration techniques were even able to control the molecular structure of the water to some level.

Eventually, the surface did become habitable. Some even ventured out to reclaim it. Only to find that a new species of man had made it their home.

Fascinated by these beings, they began to study them. Mostly observing, with occasional limited interactions. Dropping hints here and there and essentially guiding their evolution.

Now the bugs had returned and the new humans were literally knocking at the door. They knew that they could help them and that they should. The real question was how?

16.

A series of tests were run. The door appeared to be made of an unidentifiable metal. The radar would not penetrate it. So they decided to use explosives. Just as they were setting the last of the charges, several of the symbols began to light up then all at once the door opened.

Standing in the doorway was an unexceptional-looking man. He was unarmed yet looked unconcerned.

"If you would kindly stow your explosives and other weapons and follow me in an orderly fashion, I suppose we can get on with all this." Then he turned and headed back down the hall from which he had come.

Shocked beyond belief, they stood gaping for a moment. "I think we should see what he has to say." said one.

"What if it's a trap?" said another. After some discussion, they agreed their options were fairly limited and moved on through the door in search of the strange man.

The hallway led to a large chamber, well-kept, but not fancy. The man was seated in a large chair which faced a selection of other furniture. He sat patiently and motioned for them to join him.

"I suppose you all have questions? please hold them until I have said my piece." He then began to explain to them his position.

That they had indeed found salvation, albeit not in the way they desired it. He told the history of his people and how while there was no defeating the bugs, you could learn to exist in other ways.

An hour or so later they were back on the sub making the slow ascent back toward Ocean City. No one said much. Indeed, they all had a great deal to think about.

17.

Word had spread around the city of the mystery sub. Was it a rescue, reinforcements, or a new enemy? The people were terrified enough and were now demanding to know what was happening.

Safely insulated from all the calamity. The founders of Ocean City were now meeting with the scientists who had only just returned from the deep. Their discrepancy was seen as being temporarily overlooked in light of the news they had returned with. And so now the leader of Ocean City, the apparent remainder of all humanity, was faced with some decisions.

The mysterious member of the ancient race had given them a choice. They could submit to testing and evaluation to be accepted into the mysterious society, or remain in Ocean City and make a go of it.

It was decided that they would send down a group immediately and the first would consist of several board members, some of the scientists and some people from the tour sub who were inciting all the rabble-rousing.

This announcement seemed to only raise more questions from the frightened masses, but they went along with it. And so, the research sub departed early the next day. Soon they stood in the nice room, curiously observing the unremarkable man as he began to explain to them the nature of what lay ahead.

"You are all in possession of ideas," he explained.

Ideas which are unnecessary and in fact detrimental to the way of life to which we have become accustomed to living in this world for more than 100 thousand years. Many of you will not be able to let go of these, and as a result, cannot be permitted to coexist among us. those of you who can adapt will experience something the likes of which you have only dreamed possible. The rest of you will be returned to Ocean City and may continue on with your ways until well, you come to your inevitable conclusion.

Let us begin.

18.

Life above ground had become life in hell. The bugs never tired. If they did, their numbers were so vast that it did not matter. People were hungry. Many of them were scarred or burnt. Desperately sneaking about like rats in search of anything they could find.

Then the man came from Ocean City. He said they'd found a way to make room. Some sort of ancient underground human society had come to the rescue. Twice, he'd left with a larger group of people and returned alone carrying on about this ancient race of saviours.

Each group had been amazed to make it to Ocean City, much less to see it for the most part abandoned. A few people moved here and there, but it was practically a ghost town. They were led through the city, through tunnels and down elevators to the deepest part where the docks were, and then asked to board a sub.

In a room, far below Ocean City, they were individually examined. Those deemed suitable were then hooked up to a machine.

They would fall asleep and wake up in an artificially constructed reality. They were given a day to wander around and experience the thing, then had to decide to stay in or go back. Assured that their bodies would be safe and that they could return later if they wanted, many chose to stay longer in the construct. Those who returned were forced to wait a full year before they could try again. Many of them returned reluctantly and wanted to return, while others were set against it. A few even spoke out against it and tried to dissuade others from even taking the trip.

Others did take it though. It was amazing that this many people were even still alive, much less that they had all managed to find their way to Ocean City. Although it never did get crowded.

More and more people were choosing to stay in the program but how big was this place, and how were they caring for all these bodies?

19.

At some point, the massive exodus from the mountain base began to cause worry among the ranks. At first, they were glad to be rid of the excess, but now the mountain was understaffed. Soldiers were abandoning their posts. It had become an issue.

The base commander assembled a top-notch team to infiltrate the city and report back as to exactly what was going on down there.

Their arrival in Ocean City was met with a mixed crowd, most were wary of their presence, while others cheered them and begged them to stop whatever sorcery had seduced so many friends and neighbours onto that accursed submarine. Said accursed submarine was currently not on base, so they had time to listen to a few versions of the situation while they awaited its return.

When it did arrive, they boarded and forced the captain to take them back down. They entered the temple and blew open the metal door before anyone knew they were there. The captain led them to the place where they entered into the construct. Several bodies were being wheeled away on carts. The orderlies who did not normally make contact with the surface humans were shocked. The soldiers immediately opened fire and killed all but one of them.

Before they could ask him anything, however, they were all suddenly paralyzed as an invisible force caused them all to seize up and drop to the floor.

Three unexceptional-looking men entered the room.

"Clean up this mess." said the one who was apparently in charge. Upload the murderers and send their remains for storage. And send off to the cloning pool for new orderlies.

He then approached the captain and asked what he had seen.

"They all decided to stay?" he said.

"Very good, return to your ship. We'll see you tomorrow."

20.

He barely remembered having a real life, or a real body. He'd been in the simulation for well over a hundred thousand years. His life as an ocean city custodian seemed, well, like a thousand lifetimes ago.

But this was a new day. The bugs had gone back into hibernation aeons ago. The surface was again habitable. It's true that a lot of people could care less, there had always been bodies to do the work. To keep the system running smoothly, and protect it from threats. But most of the work of society was done from within the construct.

Still, they had made a huge deal about it. If it didn't suit you, they could always find somebody else. Still, he wanted to see it, to experience the real world. Where if you were cut, you would bleed, and if you died, who really knew?

Of course, his body had died ages ago. His DNA was on file though so a clone could be made for him. Or if he chose, he could pick another body, but he had decided his old body would be part of the novelty. In the construct, you could appear however you like. And change as often as you like.

He sat down in front of the machine and closed his eyes. When he awoke, everything seemed strange. He was cleaned up and dressed, then introduced to the rest of his team. Several of whom were also survivors from Ocean City.

They set out in a craft that could maneuver easily beneath the waves or above them. Ocean City was barely ruins. The oceans had revealed it during the ice age, then returned to cover it again during the thaw.

On the surface, most of the ice was gone. Green trees and plants had sprung to life all over the place. Wildlife darted here and there. And then they found what they had been looking for. A tribe of primitive-looking humans gathered around a fire. The beings looked upward in marvel and terror at the shiny floating craft that observed them. Then one of them hurled a stone.

Everything is Magic

1.

Once there was an all-powerful wizard who conquered the whole world and achieved peace. Mostly everyone was happy. He was not an evil wizard. A touch mad, but not at all evil. However, there were other wizards who were quite powerful, and they wanted to be all-powerful. They banded together and trapped him in a tall tower.

Then they began to battle and struggle amongst themselves to see who was the most powerful.

They amassed armies and fought brutal wars, pilfered resources and slaughtered countless innocents. One would rule for a spell, and then be overthrown by another and so this continued for ages.

The mad wizard did not mind his confinement. He carried on at the top of his tower, conducting experiments in magic and watching shows.

Occasionally, he would slip out unnoticed and wonder about the town of Hoghed at the foot of the tower. He would get drunk and converse with villagers as to the state of affairs in the world. He got a good laugh out of how they would declare their allegiance to one wizard or the other, and speak of how much better things were since that one had come to power. Sometimes he would ride about the town in a vehicle made of magic, randomly casting spells and curses until he became bored or tired. Then he would return to the tower and eat and watch shows until he fell asleep.

The people of Hoghed would sometimes wake up and have no idea why they had six legs, or a new house, or spoke backwards. Some of them speculated that it was the work of the wizard, as they had been led to believe he was quite evil.

A few of them got together and decided to do something about it once and for all.

2.

The tower was of course bound up in spells. No one could enter or supposedly leave its confines. They decided they would just blow it up. They brought all the powder they could scrounge from all the surrounding towns and surrounded the base with it. Then they hid in the woods and lit the fuse.

The resulting blast destroyed a good part of the town, scared the livestock, and caused more than one person to go deaf, but when the smoke cleared the tower stood. Tarnished, but unscathed.

The wizard was soaking in the tub, playing games on his device. He could see in his magic windows what the people were doing and had to laugh at the absurdity of it. It did hurt his feelings though.

He dried himself off and walked to the window overlooking the town. He could easily have repaired the destruction this foolishness had wrought. He thought it better to let them clean up their own mess.

Later inspectors from the order of the currently self-proclaimed wizard arrived to discover just what the heck was going on. The people proclaimed that the wizard had caused the destruction in an attempt to escape which they, through their valiance had thwarted.

The inspectors were sceptical but decided that measures must be taken to ensure that such things were not possible. They checked and rechecked the binding spells and found them to be stable.

Then the one who was in charge contacted the wizard, by means of a string that was run up the tower.

"Was this your doing wizard?" he said.

"Oh yes," replied the wizard. "Or rather it was my evil cat. See I had left my extra terrible explosion device on the window ledge, and she must have tipped it off over the town."

Thinking the matter was resolved, the inspectors headed out of town, back to the castle in the mountains where the other wizard resided.

The townspeople however knew it was not resolved. As did the wizard.

3.

It was not out of malice, that he turned the whole village into frogs for a day. More a gentle chastisement. Some of them even enjoyed being frogs. Of course, some of them also fell victim to cats and birds, but at the end of the day, most of them had a new respect for the wizard. They even sent up a cake, by way of a balloon, with a note saying thank you for not incinerating the lot of us.

There were a few however who were convinced that this sorcery would be the death of them all.

"Why couldn't he have changed us to squirrels?" one said. "We could have climbed up and scratched out his cursed eyes."

These malcontents conspired amongst themselves and decided that they should find yet another way to rid themselves of the wizard. What they did not know was that he was in fact in on their little conspiracy and that it was in fact his own plan to tunnel under one side of the tower causing it to fall over.

So, they set about digging. Many others tried to dissuade them pleading with them not to upset the wizard again.

"Next time he may cause it to rain serpents, or close up our bottoms till we all explode in a rain of unmentionable."

"He can't do any of that if he's smashed flat in the wreck of this building, can he?"

The wizard watched all of this in his windows. He even came down and helped dig for a spell. He wracked his brain on how he might deal with the plotters, but spare the rest of the village which meant him no harm.

Eventually, they had dug so much that it seemed impossible the tower was still standing.

"It must be the magics holding it up," said one.

"Or the wizards just waiting to drop it on our heads," said another.

Then a stranger rode into town. Wouldn't you know, he claimed to be a wizard.

4.

The stranger who claimed to be a wizard, who was actually a wizard, but not actually a stranger, stepped up to the pit they had dug and drew in a breath.

When the tower had been built, with magic, a certain stone had been used which was enchanted. It would not only, supposedly, trap the wizard inside, but also cause the building to be immovable and indestructible. The stone had been lain in the very foundation deep underground in the place he was now looking at.

He began to chant incantations whilst moving his arms and dancing about in circles. Then he clasped his hands together and thrust them at the stone and let out a bellow like a thunderclap. KAZAHHH!!!

The stone shattered into dust.

Then he stopped time. Made his way up to his rooms, gathered his things together as well as his cat, who was not evil by the way, and stuffed it all beneath his favourite hat.

As he started to leave, he suddenly felt kind of bad about the townspeople, who were about to be crushed by the falling building. Only a little bad, but enough that he took a moment to woosh some of the ones he liked out of harm's way.

Though he did love his magic car, he had a destination in mind that could only be reached by flying, so he summoned a dragon. Old friends they were, the dragon was delighted to see him.

As they were flying away, he thought of another little joke. He used the debris from the fallen tower to build a wall around the entire town so no one could leave or come in. Deciding that was just too mean, he made them a doorway, but he put it up really kind of high so it would be a terrible bother.

5.

The people of Hoghed got on well enough for a time. The story of the wizard and the wall was told enough times that no one had any clear idea of what had actually transpired.

The investigators had come, only to discover to their dismay that despite all else the wizard had apparently escaped. To where no one could say.

They built ramps and stairs up to the door on both sides, but it was still a terrible bother.

One day an especially heroic young lad decided that he should set out on a quest to find the wizard and ask that he remove the wall. Or at least lower the door. And so, he did set out, though he had no idea where to look.

The other wizards, mainly the ones in power, were all very concerned by this development. Some of them allied with each other in preparation for some reprisal. It did not come.

On the island of dragons, the wizard spent his time playing games with his dragon friend. And when he was occupied by some important dragon business or other, the wizard would just amuse himself with his games and shows. The state of the world did not much concern him anymore.

Some of the dragons were jealous, however, they did not have a magician to play games with or scratch the itchy spots beneath their scales. They told the birds who told the fish and so on until eventually it became known to the other wizards and so they set out to find him.

Soon after a ship came to Dragon Island and on it were wizards as well as a heroic young lad from Hoghed. The wizard, who wanted no part of it, bade goodbye to his dragon friend latched onto a comet and flew away.

The dragons then burned the ship and ate the men alive.

6.

Riding a comet is not as delightful as it may sound. It wasn't long until he grew tired of it and set himself down on the moon. See if anyone bothers me here, he thought, as he took off his hat and made camp.

The cat did not like the moon. Graceful as she was on the ground back home, here it had a way of slipping away if you weren't careful. Also, her milk refused to stay in the bowl. As with most trivial adversities, adjustments were made and before long it began to feel like home.

He'd built a castle of moon rocks, it had a tall tower which he ironically spent most of his time in. He made clones of himself, clones of his cat, and even clones of some moon creatures whom he found to be just precious.

A star fell nearby, curious he went out to it in his magic moon vehicle. Having never seen a star close up he became most excited.

"Are you o.k.?" he asked.

"Been better." The star replied.

And so, they became best of friends. All day they would talk and laugh and play games. He became very fond of her, though he knew she would eventually have to retake her place in the heavens.

She flat refused to let him clone her, but before she left, she shed a tear which turned to crystal. Keep this close to your heart and I will always be with you, she said. And then she left.

After that, the moon had lost its appeal to him.

He loaded his things aboard a magic rocket, waved goodbye to the clones, and set off once again.

7.

When the ship never returned from Dragon Island the wizards began to get paranoid. With no news, they could only assume it was the wizard who had been victorious, and so they expected retaliation.

They hid in their castles under the protection of powerful spells. They scryed into their mirrors and cast bones in hopes of some insight into what lay ahead. Armies were positioned and repositioned. Weapons were forged and deadly monsters were rounded up and made ready to fight.

But he never showed. No one had any idea where he might have gone or if he would ever return. They remained vigilant for a time, and after years had passed with no sign they began to relax. They resumed battling with one another, and against anyone who tried to stand against them.

When he did return, it was to a place high in the snow-covered mountains. A place where no one would ever go. He lived there for a time, just watching. He watched the wars and the injustices inflicted by men and wizards alike. He thought of the peace he had brought to this world and how it seemed the only ones who weren't happy with it had been the other wizards.

There were snow monsters who lived in the mountains. While apprehensive at first, they came to trust the magician. He taught them things and lived beside them harmoniously, despite their animal nature and savage ways. He pondered the difference between the beasts and men and realized that it was slight but prevalent. Despite the knowledge and skill of man, the beast seemed the more civilized in that they did not need to conquer or control. So long as their needs were met, they were happy. He wondered if there might be a way to accomplish the peace he had found with the monsters, back in the world of men.

The wizards meanwhile, preoccupied with wars, had not entirely forgotten the threat of his eventual return. They had set about the laying of traps. Fiendishly clever and devious in nature. They had fought hard to control the world and had no intention of letting it go easy.

8.

The years of constant warfare had taken a toll on people, and there were those who were tired of suffering under the rule of wizards. Not only were they too powerful to overthrow, but many seemed to enjoy serving one master or another believing that such leadership had allowed them to prosper.

It had also been made known that the wizards were the only defence anyone had against the return of the truly evil sorcerer and his wicked machinations. How short people's memories are.

There were those however who did remember the peaceful times. Those did concern themselves with the fate of the wizard. Had he been killed as some thought, exiled somewhere else? If not. Why did he not return to battle the wizards and return the peace?

Time passed and as the wizards grew more powerful, the people became more and more discontent with their rule. A resistance began. They knew little success at first. They were persecuted harshly, but they persevered.

The wizard watched all of this from his solitude in the mountains. He thought perhaps there was hope for man after all.

If they were willing to fight to free themselves of this oppression, if they really did desire peace, maybe they deserved another chance.

The people of Hoghed were going about their lives as usual, when suddenly there was a rumbling sound. Suddenly the air was alive with hurtling stones. It happened swiftly, yet was a wonder to behold. The wall around the town was gone. Once more in the center of the village, stood the tallest tower any of them had ever seen.

9.

The leaders of the town met with the wizard. They were happy to learn that he had no plans to destroy them. However, when he announced his intentions to remove the other wizards from power, the mood changed considerably.

They were terrified, and decided that things weren't so bad as they were, and couldn't he just return to wherever he'd come from and forget this foolishness?

But no, he had made up his mind. For too long he had watched and done nothing. It made him sad that they could not imagine a better way for themselves they would have to be shown.

The other wizards meanwhile, had become aware of his return. They had of course readied their armies and secured their castles. They had sent out spies, and they had employed even the men of the town to be complicit in the plot to destroy the wizard.

They surrounded the town and began to invade, only to find that at a certain distance, the town grew no closer. For days they marched on the town, and still there it was, just at the edge of their sight. Too far for their cannons.

Then the wizard appeared on the field. He begged them all, not to turn on their masters, but to turn around. Go home, tend the fields and the shops. To die on this field would serve no one.

Some tried to leave, but of course, they were not allowed. The spells of the wizards had set in their minds. Those who intended to flee were branded cowards and traitors and were cut down.

Enraged the wizard called up a ferocious storm. Battlements were blown apart by the winds, and water came up from the ground to make escape impossible. The trees and the air then came alive and devoured all who still stood until he faced only the wizards.

Even together they weren't a match for him and so they fled. He cursed them as cowards and turned them inside out. One by one, he cursed them with horns and hooves and disfigurements, but foolishly he allowed them to live.

10.

So for a while, there was peace. They melted down all the weapons and used the metals to build tools and boats. They built buildings and made art. There was plenty to be had for all and mostly everyone was happy.

But isn't there always that lot of malcontents who just revel in ruining things for everyone? And of course, the banished wizards were happy to give them what they wanted. They began to gather followers and to plot and plan.

Meanwhile, the rest of the world carried on, oblivious to these malicious intentions. True there were quarrels and skirmishes, but for the most part, these were resolved peacefully. The wizard had taken to roaming the countryside, seeking out rare beasties and basking in cosmic radiation.

He met a grass fairy who said she could see the future. She told him to beware. That a shadow hung over him, a child's shadow. And that shadow was doom. Knowing how fairies can be, he paid her no mind and continued on with his travels.

He met giants and trolls, crossed dimensions with a mystic, even travelled in time and witnessed the birth of the world. After a while, he returned to his tower and rested.

It came to his attention that a boy had been taken from the village. He was being held by one of the banished wizards in a cell in his castle. Of course, he went there straight away meaning to set things right, but it was a trick. The cursed wizards fell upon him with everything they had, and when he had mostly defeated them, he went to the cell to rescue the boy.

But the boy had been cursed. He was the core of the plot and as soon as he opened the door to the cell he knew, but it was too late. The boy was cursed with death. To all who touched or even saw him.

He thought of the fairy, the wretched imp, he thought of the star and he thought of the dragon. And then he thought no more.

11.

It started out like a dream and then continued on as a dream for some time. Eventually, it occurred to him that he had been dreaming for too long. Also, it was like no dream he'd had before. It was all much too real, yet simultaneously unreal. And it had nothing, or perhaps everything to do with magic.

He continued to do what he imagined was walking, until he realized that he could not be walking, as he had no legs. Not sure of what he was seeing, for he had no eyes. Thinking how strange this was seemed stranger still in that he had no mind with which to think it.

He came upon a thing which seemed to be a turtle. They communicated in some type of way he did not understand, but was effective in that he began to. The turtle thing sang to him in a way that required no sound, and he was able to understand it without hearing. He began to feel at ease. All that had troubled him began to congeal into a sense of warmth. With a feeling of oneness, in an instant, he understood things he never thought he would things that mattered and things that didn't, and why they did or did not.

He felt himself being drawn to a place not far away. A place where he could rest forever, or feel good, or not feel. A place seemingly made real by the very thought of it. It would be insane to resist it. Every reason he could think of just melted away, and the place became closer and closer.

Then for some reason he himself could neither explain nor understand, he did resist it. He resisted with all the strength and magic that he possessed. For a moment it seemed futile, but then just as he was about to have to give up, something changed, he felt himself falling. A sort of reality began to form around him. Not the one we know, but similar. He fell into a vessel that was much like a body, but not quite. He found he could open his eyes and so he did. Before him stood another sort of plain, unfinished-looking humanoid who was looking at him with some astonishment.

"Why did you do that?" he said.

12.

Unsure of what he had done, much less why he had done it, he answered as best he could.

"I don't know."

The man glared at him, paced around a bit, and then sat down in a chair he was sure wasn't there before. He then realized that he was now seated in a similar chair.

"This is unprecedented, you have served your purpose. Now you are to be absorbed back into the life force, it is just the way of things. Why have you resisted?"

"But I must save that boy, I must destroy the other wizards for good and bring peace."

"These things are beyond you now your time is done. You have died and now your life force is needed to create something else. What was you can now live on in my mind as a thought, if that is your desire, or you can cease to exist? But you needn't worry about the troubles of the living world. You are dead."

He thought on this, deciding he could not argue or barter, the being could neither be bribed nor tricked he had no option but to play along.

"Very well," he said, "Do what you will. I will not resist."

The being regarded him curiously.

"If I send you back, would you do something for me?"

"If I can, then I suppose I must," he answered.

"I would like you to rid the world of magic. It has been fun, but I feel it has run its course. Not only is it grossly misused by some to control others, but what has happened here I'm afraid can never be allowed to happen again. So yes, I will send you back. You may continue your own agenda, but before you return to me again. You must gather up all of the magic that exists and destroy it."

Before he could answer he felt himself being wooshed away by an unseen current. He then fell fast asleep.

13.

"It was like watching a show. How could he not have seen the plot? He had underestimated their treachery and paid for it, with his life. How then was he watching himself climb the stairs to the tower?" "Wait," he shouted just as he was about to open the door to the cell. But suddenly he was not watching.

He looked down at his hands, they seemed real enough. Had it been some sort of vision? He would think about it later. For now, the boy.

He cast a spell for darkness and bound it to the boy. Then shrunk him down and placed him into a vial, which he promptly stashed under his hat.

He could sense the other wizards drawing near. He wanted to destroy them where they stood, but it wouldn't do to further endanger the life of the boy. Best he be removed from the equation entirely. He confounded them all to chase their own tails, whilst he set about bewitching a carpet.

As they grovelled about like dogs, he made good his escape with the boy tucked safely away.

He returned to the tower in Hoghed. He then summoned his books and inquired as to the death spell. It was an old and sinister magic. He could reverse it, but it would take a toll. He and the boy would be irreversibly bound. Still, confident that it was the only righteous course of action, he began laying out his things and making various preparations for the rite.

It was a tricky thing. It involved fairies and spirits and incense and incantations and even some lightning. In the end, though, it had worked. The boy was cured, and his size was restored. And he was ever so grateful.

He pledged himself to the wizard, for he was an orphan with no real home or family. The wizard could see no harm and agreed to let him stay on as a servant. He could begin with cleaning up this mess. Then he went to take a nap, for he was tired and tomorrow would not be easy.

14.

Of the evil wizards it could be said that in fact, some were more evil than others. That said, they were all evil enough and dangerous enough that it was decided that none of them should be allowed to live.

It could also be said that some were more powerful than others, and so he saw fit to start with the least of these and to work his way up.

Some of the more foolish ones had decided it would be best to strike when least expected. He dispatched them before breakfast.

The first snuck in as a rodent, and his cat got that one. The second came as a bird, and he also went to the cat. The third, a little more clever came as a dog, but the wizard was even more sharp and saw through the ruse. He threw him a cursed bone which first revealed him and then incapacitated him just long enough for the wizard to regard the cat who already appeared quite full, so he just turned him into a pig which he promptly slaughtered.

He then set out to find the others. They were spread out but eventually, he tracked them all down. He attacked them with magic, he attacked them with the sword. Threw one into a volcano, and sent one hurtling into the sun. He fought them with water and fought them with fire. He took injury here and there, but nothing he could not heal with his own spells.

Finally, only 2 remained. Himself, and the evillest and most powerful of all the other wizards.

He sat waiting at a long table high in his own castle. They sat down and shared a meal, they talked of many things. Including the being, and his proposition that the time of magic had ended.

"If the time of magic is over, perhaps we should finish this another way." The evil wizard said.

And so, they duelled with weapons, of course, he tried to cheat and use magic, but in the end, his head was separated from the rest of him and all the magic in the world rested in the hands of the one all-powerful wizard.

15.

So for a while, all was right with the world. Fishes carried on being fishes and snow monsters carried on being snow monsters. The wizard went back to his shows and games, and the boy was happy with dusting and sweeping and keeping track of the clones.

No one seemed to miss the magic after all the ordeals with the evil wizards, they were happy just tending their fields and putting on the occasional play. They replaced it with rules and facts, laws science, and something called religion. The elves and fairies grew bored and moved on to other worlds.

After a while, people forgot about the magic. Many believed it was only stories and that even the wizard who had grown quite old, was only powerful in that he had a tall castle and a servant to run his errands.

Sometimes the boy who was also older and not really a boy anymore, would ask him why he no longer did magic. He mostly ignored these inquiries, but one day he was fairly drunk and he related the story of the arrangement he had struck with the source being.

Of course, he was glad it had happened that way for he had been rescued from a terrible fate, but also it seemed unfair. In his heart he had wished to learn from the wizard and to one day become a master of sorcery himself.

He began to secretly study from the many books and crystals that the wizard kept hidden away in the tower. In time he began to develop some skills.

Many years later, he decided to show the wizard what he had learned and ask him to make him an apprentice.

The wizard was hesitant, he did not see how this could appease his arrangement, but he did like the boy and had always wanted an apprentice. He figured, what could be the harm in showing him a thing or two?

16.

After some years had passed, and much knowledge had been passed, the wizard began to grow very old. While his apprentice seemed wise and capable, the old wizard began to wonder if he hadn't made a mistake in deciding to train him.

He thought perhaps it was the being who had made the mistake. For if a wizard was both wise and capable, then what could be the harm?

The apprentice also thought long on these things. He believed with all his heart that as long as he used his magic in ways that were beneficial to all perhaps things could be different. He loved magic. It had nearly killed him, but it had also saved him. It had rid the world of the evil overlords who misused its gifts, and it had made him strong and respected among the people he watched over.

Also, there were still a few who longed for it. They were jealous of the wizard and his apprentice. They wanted to learn magic for themselves. The wizard saw this and then realized the danger which he had provoked.

They began to practice lost arts, to summon fairies from the places they had gone to. And from them fashioned rudimentary spells, mostly harmless but it was the beginning of something.

The two sages sat down to discuss what, if anything should be done about it.

"Who are we to say what is right for everyone," asked the apprentice.

"And what are we to do when they rise up against us," replied the wizard.

Confounded, the wizard went for a ride in his magic vehicle. He rode it far out on the plain and made a picnic. He gazed at his crystal and asked the star what path he might follow. Apparently, she was busy with celestial matters. He wished he might speak with the being again. He crossed all the dimensions and planes but found no sign. Then he fell asleep and had a vision.

17.

In his vision, he was sitting in a most comfortable chair. Before him on a giant screen, he watched the history and future of the world. At some point, he realized that next to him was the being he had met near the life source.

The being said nothing. Merely sat watching the progression of events with a casual disinterest.

Eventually, the wizard leaned over and asked, "What is the point of all this?"

To this he did not reply, he sort of shrugged and made a shushing gesture.

Shortly after the wizard awakened in the field, still unsure of what was expected of him.

He returned home to find that his apprentice had begun to teach magic to some of the people. He thought it could be something to cause problems, but then again it would apparently work itself out in time. He went up to his tower and slept.

He was awakened by his apprentice who seemed rather shaken.

"What have I done," he said. I taught them magic and they have used it to awaken monsters!

The old wizard gazed into his windows and saw that it was true. Throughout the lands, novice magicians had summoned creatures of all manner and they were romping from here to there laying a path of destruction in their wake.

"It is what they wanted," said the wizard. "Let them deal with it." and then he went back to sleep.

The apprentice did his best to round up and banish the fiends, but despite his best efforts he was but one wizard and not an all-powerful one.

He enlisted the help of some of his more advanced students and together they set out to heal the land.

18.

A vast army of trolls, wyverns, ghouls, and wyrms had infested the face of the world, evading and escapading without care or cause. A new breed of sorcerer had appeared, neither evil nor good. They did magic just for the sake of it. Toying with forces they did not begin to understand. Testing the sheer limits of chaos, attempting to undo the very fabric of existence through foolery and hijinks.

The wizard was quite amused by this. In all his time he had worked hard to control the forces, to control his own impulses. He had been conditioned it seemed to fear just the outcome that was happening all around him. Everyone was not enjoying it, that's true, but was there really such a scenario in which everyone could be equally satisfied?

He watched with hopeful pride as his young apprentice worked in vain to curb the torrent, he had unknowingly unleashed. The magicians he had trained also acted nobly and worked with diligence. The pranksters it seemed were too many, however, and too clever.

The dark druids had pooled their knowledge, and aligned with the faeries. They had birthed an enchantment which made everything magic. There were toads going around changing things into people. Lightning burst forth from the ground. Cats were chasing dogs, and Leviathan was swimming across the sky.

It was all completely out of hand, and it was marvellous. While some were hiding in caves and wailing, others danced naked in the chaos. Everything was unchained. For all that was destroyed in the revelry, it was the birth of a true freedom the likes of which the world had never known.

The wizard sat high in his tower watching. While he was amused, he had to shake his head sadly. He knew it could not last. He had seen it.

19.

So for a while, the world was filled with magic. It was ruled by none. People were free as well as monsters of all kinds.

People grew lazy, they had stopped doing things on their own. They used magic for everything.

Building ships and houses, and growing food, they used it to travel, to solve quarrels. They used it to entertain themselves and occasionally to fight off monsters.

The wizard was walking one day in the clouds. He met a space lord. They got to talking and realized that they knew the same star. So, they got into his ship and went to visit her.

She was hanging about near the rings of Saturn. Just dancing around and singing a tune.

She was happy to see the wizard for they had been such good friends. He told her about the snow monsters and the evil wizards. About the source and the being and what had been said. She seemed amused for a while, but soon became bored and floated off to explore the outer worlds. He then realized that the space lord had also deserted him and he wasn't sure how he would get back if at all.

He considered just staying there. The view was nice, but he missed his apprentice, his cat and his clones. He waited for a comet or an asteroid to pass by, but got tired of waiting so he just punched a hole in the spacetime and was back in the tower in time for supper.

He was joined by his apprentice and a few of his students. They were tired from battling golems and chimaeras and they complained to the wizard that all of this magic had become a real pain in the neck. Then they used spells to clear the table and wash the cookery.

After supper, he went down to the tavern. He didn't stay long; it was the same old scene. He returned to the tower and readied for sleep, but was surprised to find someone sitting in the chair gazing out of his window.

It was the source being.

20.

For a while, they just sit and stare out from the window. The view is nice. The weather is nice. In the distance screaming can be heard. Likely some abomination or other has made its way into the village and is orchestrating some manner of horrific deed.

The silence is like a game. Should it be broken, or not? And if it is then by what, and by who. His mind reels with both statements and questions. At the same time, he wonders about the being. How like him is it? does it think like him, and if it does what is it thinking? What does it expect of him?

"Do you like magic?" the being asks after what seems a very long time.

"Of course," replied the wizard.

"Is it essential?"

"It's true, most things can be accomplished without it, so I suppose not."

"That is a good answer. You are quite wise for a man, yet you are wrong. It is essential. Magic is all there is really. The using of it differs from thing to thing, but stripped down to the very base of things is a tiny bit of magic wrapped in layer upon layer of different magic. Of course, none of this is real. Not in any sense that you, in all your ageless wisdom would understand. It is but a thought that I have had, or am having it is a dream in the mind of a dreamer. An idea for a song in the mind of a bard. I could go on, but you catch my meaning."

The wizard scratched his beard and made a puzzled look.

"But I thought it was your wish that all magic would come to an end."

If that were my wish, then it would be so. I only wished to see what you might make of my demand. And I am intrigued by your observation of the outcome. It appears this world has been overrun.

"Yes," he said. "It would appear so."

When he awoke the next day, all magic was gone and he was a simple farmer with an unbelievable story to tell to anyone who would listen.